Sesame Street Start-to-Read Books™
help young children take a giant step into reading.
The stories have been skillfully written, designed,
and illustrated to provide funny, satisfying
reading experiences for the child just starting out.
Let Big Bird, Bert and Ernie, Oscar the Grouch,
and all the Sesame Street Muppets get your child
into reading early with these wonderful stories!

Library of Congress Cataloging-in-Publication Data:
Smith, Jennifer, 1943–   . Grover and the new kid. (A Sesame Street start-to-read book) SUMMARY: Grover helps a new boy in school understand the importance of getting along with others. [1. Behavior—Fiction. 2. Friendship—Fiction. 3. School—Fiction. 4. Puppets—Fiction] I. Cooke, Tom, ill. II. Children's Television Workshop. III. Title. IV. Series: Sesame Street start-to-read books.   PZ7.S6514Gr   1987   [E]   86-42965   ISBN: 0-394-88519-8 (trade); 0-394-98519-2 (lib. bdg.)

Manufactured in the United States of America   2 3 4 5 6 7 8 9 0

Grover and the New Kid

by Jennifer Smith • illustrated by Tom Cooke

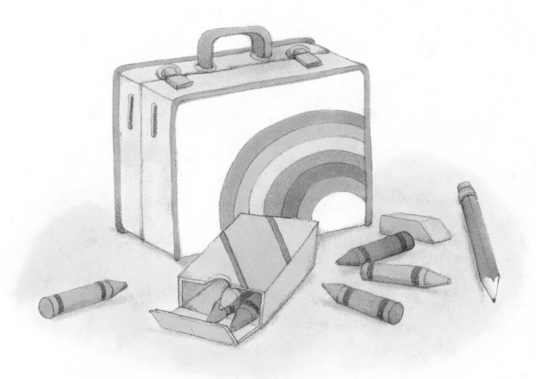

Featuring Jim Henson's Sesame Street Muppets

Random House/Children's Television Workshop

Grover liked school.
He liked his room.
He liked his teacher.
He liked the children
in his class.

One day a new boy came
to Grover's school.
"This is Barry," said the teacher.
"Barry is going to be in our class."
"It is hard to be the new kid,"
Grover said to himself.
"I will help Barry.
I will be his friend."

one
two
three

Grover said, "Hi, Barry.
My name is Grover."
Barry said, "Hi!
Look what I have!"
Barry took a little car
out of his pocket.

"Oh, what a cute little car!
May I play with it?" asked Grover.
Barry shook his head.
"No," he said.
"Oh," said Grover.
"I understand."

Grover showed Barry
the clay cupboard.

He shared his crayons
with Barry.

He helped Barry
find the bathroom.

He even gave Barry
one of his cookies
at milk time.
But Barry never once
said thank you.

Soon it was story time.

Everyone sat in a circle.

They listened to the teacher read
"Goldilocks and the Three Bears."

Everyone was very quiet—
everyone but Barry.
"Please be quiet and listen,"
said the teacher.
Barry kept talking.

After story time everyone went
to the playground.
"Let's go on the slide," said Barry.
"Okay," said Grover.
Grover got in line behind Sam.
But Barry ran to the front
and pushed in front of Molly.

Barry climbed up the ladder
and stood at the top of the slide.
"Hey, Grover!" he called.
"Look at me!"

Molly started up the ladder.
"Barry did not wait his turn,"
she said. "That is not nice.
Who does he think he is!"
Grover said, "He is just new.
It is hard to be the new kid.
Do not be mad at him."

Back inside Grover showed Barry
the wooden puzzles.
There was a farm puzzle,
an airport puzzle,
and a circus puzzle.
Truman had the farm puzzle.

"I want that one,"
said Barry.
He grabbed it from Truman.

At lunch Grover was the only one
who sat with Barry.
The others talked about Barry.
"Barry doesn't wait his turn,"
said Molly.

"Barry doesn't say please
or thank you," said Truman.
"Barry reminds me of someone—
someone rude," said Sam.
"Who?" asked Molly.
"Goldilocks!" said Sam.
They all laughed and laughed.

After lunch Grover painted
a picture with a yellow sun,
a red house, and a little blue car.
He stood back and looked
at his picture.
It looked good!
Grover was proud of his painting.

Then Barry came over.
He showed Grover his painting.
It was a picture of a fire truck.
"That is very nice, Barry,"
said Grover. "Do you like mine?"

"You need a fire truck
in your picture," Barry said.
And he picked up a brush
and painted a big red fire truck
next to the little blue car.

"I do not want a fire truck
in my painting!" shouted Grover.
"You are not nice to anyone."
And Grover walked away from Barry.
Barry looked surprised.

Grover sat all by himself
and looked out the window.
He did not want to paint anymore.
He did not want to look at books.
He did not want to do anything.

Suddenly a little toy car
ran into Grover's foot.
"Do you want to play
with my car, Grover?"
Barry asked shyly.
"I'm sorry about your painting.
I forgot how to be nice today."

"I know," said Grover.

He smiled.

"Let's play with your car together."

Soon it was time to clean up.

Molly washed the paint brushes.

Sam picked up the clay.

Truman stacked the puzzles.

Grover put away the blocks.

And Barry helped everyone!

After school Grover and Barry
walked home together.
"I was afraid to come
to school today," said Barry.
"I know," said Grover.
"It is hard to be the new kid."

At the corner Grover and Barry
waved good-bye.
"See you tomorrow!" said Grover.
"See you tomorrow!" said Barry.
"I am glad you are my friend."